Number Nine

Dorling Kinderlsey
www.dk.com

Editor Fiona Munro
Designer Lisa Hollis

Published in Great Britain in 1997
by Dorling Kindersley Limited, 9 Henrietta St, London WC2E 8PS
This edition published in 2000

2 4 6 8 10 9 7 5 3 1

A CIP catalogue record for this book is available from the British Library.

ISBN 0-7513-6709-5

Color reproduction by DOT Gradations
Printed in Hong Kong by Wing King Tong

Number Nine

COLIN AND JACQUI HAWKINS

Dorling Kindersley

“I love the sea, and it loves me!” said Number Nine.

Number Nine lived in a tall wooden house. It had nine yellow windows and an orange roof. Number Nine’s house was right by the sea.
It was the ninth house in Numbertown.
The address was 9, Number Lane.

9

Number Nine was a sailor who loved the sea.

Every morning,
he fed his nine pet
seagulls and his
nine pet crabs.

In his house,
Number Nine
had nine
ships in nine
bottles,

nine old
anchors
and nine
brass mugs.

Although Number Nine was the best sailor in Numbertown, he was the worst gardener.
"Nothing ever grows in my garden," he said sadly.

"It's because you're too salty," laughed the other Numberlies.
"Flowers don't like salt," they giggled.
"Try growing seaweed!"

Oh dear !

One day, Number Nine was sailing along in his boat when he saw something bobbing in the sea.
"What's this?" he said as he fished an old bottle out of the water.
Inside the bottle was an old map.
"It's a map of lost Lolly Island," he said excitedly.
"I'll set sail tomorrow!"

"I love the sea, and it loves me!" sang Number Nine.

A treasure map !

The next day, all the Numberlies helped Number Nine load his boat with food for the long journey. They packed nine breakfasts, nine lunches and nine suppers.

"You're off to sea!" said Number Three.

The little boat sailed off as all the other Numberlies waved goodbye.

"It's a long way to Lolly Island," said Number Nine to his jolly little boat, as they bobbed along.

Splish! Splosh!

They sailed across the sea for nine sunny days and nine starry nights.

"I love the sea, and it loves me!" sang Number Nine.

Zzzzz
zzzz.

At last, Number Nine saw
Lolly Island on the horizon.

"Land ahoy!"

he cried.

Nine minutes later,
Number Nine reached the sandy beach.
"Hi," said nine cheeky birds,
carrying nine lollipops in their beaks.
"Can I have a lolly?" asked Number Nine.

"No, no! Find where they grow!"

sang the cheeky birds as they flew away.

"How can I find where the lollies grow?" wondered Number Nine.

"We know where they grow!"

said a cheeky voice.

Number Nine looked up. Nine giggling monkeys grinned down at him.

"Don't monkey around," said Number Nine. "Where **do** the lollies grow?"

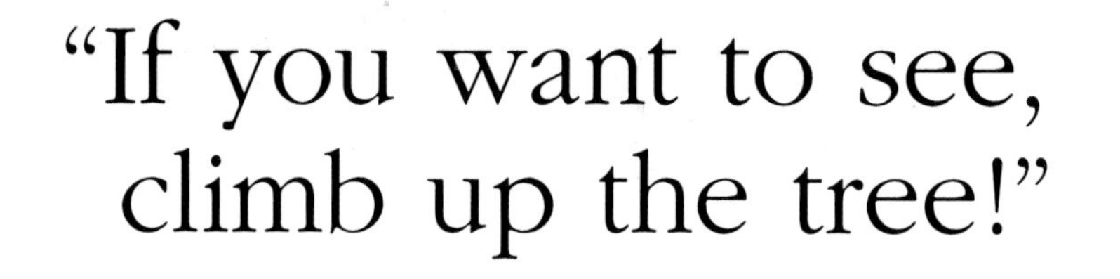

"If you want to see,
climb up the tree!"

laughed the nine monkeys.

Number Nine climbed up the tall tree until he reached the top. "This is where the lollies grow!" said Number Nine. "Lollies grow on trees!" The monkeys helped Number Nine to pack his boat with nine lollies, ready for the trip home.

"Back to the sea for me!"

said Number Nine.

I love lollies !
How jolly !

After nine days and nine nights, Number Nine arrived safely back in Numbertown. He planted nine lolly sticks in his garden.

All the Numberlies laughed, but nine days later nine little lolly trees had grown.

"What a jolly lolly garden!"

said Number Nine.

All the Numberlies agreed with him!

Look !
Clever me !

Bye!